Gorilla Warfare

Gorilla Warfare

James Quinn

Copyright (C) 2017 James Quinn
Layout design and Copyright (C) 2017 Creativia
Published 2016 by Creativia
Book design by Creativia (www.creativia.org)
Edited by Simone Beaudelaire
Cover art by Cover Mint

This book is a work of fiction. Names, characters, places, and incidents are the product of the author's imagination or are used fictitiously. Any resemblance to actual events, locales, or persons, living or dead, is purely coincidental.

All rights reserved. No part of this book may be reproduced or transmitted in any form or by any means, electronic or mechanical, including photocopying, recording, or by any information storage and retrieval system, without the author's permission.

FOR ALL MY CHILDREN
E, Z, J, A
YOU ARE THE MOST PRECIOUS THINGS
XXXX

Also by James Quinn

A Game for Assassins
The Christmas Assassin
Sentinel Five

The events of the novella "Gorilla Warfare" take place over one night in 1981 in Glasgow, Scotland.
The story is set some seven years after the events of Book 3 of the Redaction Chronicles: Rogue Wolves. While there are some character references to the previous books, this novella is a standalone and can be read independently of the main novels.
J.Q

Grief is the price we pay for love
Queen Elizabeth II

Beware of him that is slow to anger; for when it is long coming, it is the stronger when it comes, and the longer kept. Abused patience turns to fury.
Francis Quarles

Contents

Chapter One: The Shootout at Struans Bar	1
Chapter Two: Inferno	5
Chapter Three: Torture is Torture	14
Chapter Four: Jojo	22
Chapter Five: A Night in the City	27
Chapter Six: The Gathering of the Clan	32
Chapter Seven: The Bridge	39
Chapter Eight: Hannah	46
Chapter Nine: The Big Man	56
Acknowledgements	59
A Message from James Quinn	60
About the Author	63

Chapter One

The Shootout at Struans Bar

6.10 pm - Struan's Bar, Glasgow, November 1981

It was dark outside when the little killer came into the bar blasting. He was only there for answers, not to ask questions.

The fleshy-faced bartender, a tough scot from Dunfermline, had a brief moment to register the door calmly swinging open and a short figure emerging dressed in a dark suit, white shirt, dark tie, black leather gloves and sunglasses. The most remarkable thing about the well-dressed visitor was the pistol grip pump action shotgun attached to a one point sling looped around his shoulder. He looked like he knew his way around it comfortably.

The bartender, with reactions he wouldn't have given himself credit for in his more lucid moments, made a fast grab for the old .38 revolver underneath the bar. He never made it. The killer's first blast took him full in the chest, sending him hurtling back into the bottles, glasses and optics of the bar. The BOOM caused the rest of the of the bar to either flinch or swing into combative action. Hands instinctively started to reach into the small of the backs or down to undefined weapons tucked into waistbands.

There were twelve in total, all male, all tough looking and all of the criminal class who had been a part of the Glasgow underworld since they were teenagers. As of that night they were dead men walking. There was the rack of the slide and the inevitable boom of the killer's weapon. He knocked them down one after the other like bowling pins. Never stopping, never standing still, but not running either, he ambled at a steady pace along the length of the bar, moving and firing, racking and shooting. Bodies quickly dropped or were flung aside by the rounds from the pump action shotgun and quite often two targets would be taken in the same blast, either from buckshot or solid shot rounds. Two men in the last booth, both dressed in expensive business suits – they could have been accountants or solicitors – took cover behind the leather-backed seats as they searched for their personal weapons in shoulder holsters.

"Yeh fucker," cried one. It was the last words he ever spoke as the shotgun blast took his head off his shoulders; the second boom removed the other man's pelvis, causing him to splay on the floor like a rag doll, his legs now useless. A second blast to the chest stopped his screaming.

With the targets in front of him either dead or dying and no longer a threat, the little killer pivoted on his heels, the shotgun turning with him like the turret on a tank seeking out an available target. The room was a mass of red gore, shattered glass and moaning in agony. What had once been a private bar had been turned into a massacre within seconds, smelling of cheap whiskey, stale beer and blood.

A shattering noise resounded from the kitchen in the back. Someone had knocked over a pan by the sounds of it and it had clattered to the floor, giving away the person's position. The little killer moved cautiously from the small corridor and into the kitchen, the barrel of the shotgun leading the way. A small elderly man wielding a meat cleaver stood in the centre, shivering with the fright.

"Drop it. Don't think about it. Just do it. Don't make me ask you twice," said the little killer, the barrel of the shotgun pointed dead centre at the cook's head. The cook blinked twice, nodded and then dropped the cleaver onto the tile floor.

"Where is Conor McLachlan?"

The cook looked from the face of the killer to the black hole of the end of the shotgun barrel. Both were unforgiving. He could feel the sweat running down his neck.

"I dinna…know…"

The rack of the shotgun instantly changed his mind. "He doesn't come here, he prefers the fancy clubs. This is just for the lads to hang out here…I swear I dinna know!!! I beg yeh.…"

The little killer reflected on the answer. The cook was probably telling the truth. This bar was just the watering hole and meeting place for the members of the gang. No "civilians" would be allowed to enter, nor would they want to, probably.

"I believe you," said the little killer.

The cook let out a cautious sigh of relief, and then the shotgun blast took him square in the face.

The killer walked out of the service entrance at the back of the bar and into the dark alleyway. It stank of rotting vegetables and old beer bottles. Almost instantly, at the other end of the alleyway, a pair of headlights came to life and then the vehicle started to amble forward. The car, a jet black 1970's Jaguar X6, looked in the dark of the night like a panther prowling its terrain as it drew up next to him and a small, weasley-looking man in a matching dark suit and tie got out. It was Jojo McKay, the killer's "squire. "Everything go alright, Mister Grant? No problems, boss?"

Gorilla Grant shook his head, a mask of fury still stamped on his face from his recent executions. "No problems, Jojo. Let's move it. We still have much work to do tonight. You have everything ready for the next job?"

"Absolutely. I've got it all at the lock up."

"Then let's make a start," said Gorilla Grant, unhooking the sling of the shotgun from his shoulder and placing it carefully into the rear of the Jaguar before climbing in himself. Jojo closed the door behind his boss and scurried round to the driver's side. He liked it when the boss was in a good mood, when his jobs went well. These days, nobody liked to upset Gorilla Grant, especially if those who wanted to keep their kneecaps in the same place. Jojo was Gorilla's man, had been for the past few years. Whenever the boss had an important "gig," Jojo was there to help, get everything sorted, get all the gear in place. They worked well together. Oh yes, Gorilla and Jojo went back a long time, and now they had had everything that they would need for the next job in Gorilla Grant's little overnight battle plan. Chains, padlocks, explosives and petrol... above all petrol. Tonight, Gorilla and Jojo were going to set the town ablaze.

Chapter Two

Inferno

7.00pm – Cambuslang, Glasgow

What was left of the building had once been a three-story property on the junction of Main Street and Greenlees Road. The downstairs had been a women's clothes shop unit, while the upstairs had once been offices for a firm of accountants. It had been an unremarkable building in a busy row of commercial premises. Two years ago, the current property owners had given their tenants three months' notice to move out. These days, to the casual eye, it was merely another empty property lying unused. Most people passed by without giving it a second glance. It was a sign of the times, thanks to the witch in Parliament. Unemployment, loss of hope and despair were normal here in the North.

However, the property wasn't all it seemed. The casual observer wouldn't have noticed the high-quality locks protecting it, the metal grill shutters on the front to stop thieves breaking in (and also to stop people seeing in) and nobody would certainly have noticed the tough looking "minders" who took shifts sitting inside the property with only a kettle, a radio and a sawn-off shotgun for company. It was in fact the safe house and stash for the drug pipeline run by the McLachlan crime family. The drugs would be moved into the city, usually via the docks, and then stored in a discreet, armed and safe environment, namely this out of business property on Greenlees Road.

At 6pm there was an estimated street value of drugs totalling nearly three million pounds located in its safe room, expected to net a profit for the McLachlans of almost three times that much once it was cut down and passed out to the dealers and the addicts. An hour later, the property and the drugs inside had gone up in flames.

First there had been the smell of sulphur and then the homemade bombs had ignited, not so much an explosion but a slow burn that had taken the two "minders" inside by surprise. Whatever had been placed inside those explosive devices had been powerful enough to engulf the property in minutes and had spread quickly up through the rear and onto the main staircase at the back. At the same time, a similar device had been pushed under the gap between the shutters in the front. Thirty seconds later, it too had ignited and had set about burning into the shop front before working its way up the building.

The men inside had been trapped. All exits were either locked from the outside or had suddenly become a wall of fire, and it hadn't taken long before the minders had succumbed to smoke inhalation. By 6.30pm, the building, front and back, was an inferno. Passersby on the way home in the dark were treated to a spectacular event as the building became engulfed. A series of loud bangs and pops could be heard from inside. Fire service sirens blared. They would spend most of that night trying to extinguish the blaze, as it turned out, unsuccessfully.

By that time the damage had already been done. The property had been gutted, two men had died and the biggest drug pipeline stash in Scotland had gone up in flames.

Hit two had been completed.

7.45pm – Penthouse Apartment, Folsom Shipping Warehouse, James Watt Street, Glasgow

The girl lay face down, her mouth pushed into the pillow, her screams muffled. On top of her naked body, the man, his open shirt revealing his tattooed chest and his trousers rolled down around his thighs, pumped into her forcefully. With each thrust the girl whimpered in pain. She had been with this "client" before; many times. She knew she would be sore for days. He liked to hurt the girls here. She also knew there was no point in complaining. When the "big man's" nephew wanted something, he took it and he didn't care who or what he hurt in the process. She just prayed he would cum soon and then it would be over… at least for another few days.

She could feel his weight more on top of her now. He increased his speed, thrust more violently, his panting heavy. Soon it would be over… soon. The jarring peal of the telephone in the corner broke his rhythm.

"Fuck!" said Conor McLachlan, irritated, as he pulled himself out of the girl, climbed off and pulled up his trousers. He was a tall, thin man in his early 20s. His red hair and pale blue eyes sat above a cruel slash of a sneer. The girl made to get up and get dressed, but he stopped her with the harsh Glasgow bark of his voice. "YOU stay put! I'm not finished with you yet, lassie…. not by a long shot."

He strode across the well-furnished apartment and answered the telephone. "Aye," he said, his voice now back in control.

"It's me."

Conor knew "me" meant the policeman his uncle had bought and paid for over many years. The man played an integral part of the family's continuing operation in the criminal underworld.

"We have a problem, Conor. Several problems, actually. I think you should come down here," said the policeman.

"You feckin serious? I've got a wee lassie on the go here! Whatever it is, YOU sort it out. That's why my uncle pays you for…"

"Someone has torched the den. It's been incinerated along with the stash inside. It's all gone."

"Wha…? You kidding me…? That's over three mil worth of product," snarled Conor.

"That's not all, Conor. Someone walked into Struan's bar tonight and gunned down most of Jamie McCoist's crew. There was only one survivor and he's balancing between life and death at the minute."

Conor McLachlan's eyes widened. Jamie McCoist ran a team of heavies for his uncle's organisation on the Clyde. They specialised in strong arm work, armed robbery and punishment beatings. They were the enforcers of the organisation. They were hard men, not easily taken.

"Fuck!"

"So you see why I think it's a good idea that you get your trousers on?"

"I'm on my way. I'll meet you at the usual place. Get me anything you have, anything you know," said Conor hanging up the phone. His hand shook. Christ, he needed to get a grip on this before his uncle found out. Conor McLachlan had been entrusted with running his uncle's business while he was "away." He heard the girl, rising once more and getting dressed. He turned, snarling at her. "Oy, you cunt… where you think you're going? I said I'm nah finished with you yet. Get back on that bed and you take what I'm gonna give you."

He needed to get his frustrations out and hurt someone, and this whore was the way to help him clear his thoughts. He would enjoy this. He always did.

He arrived down by the river less than 45 minutes later. He'd finished with the girl, slapped her around a bit, grabbed a revolver from his cupboard and put on a clean suit. He had to make a show for the boyos; he was, after all, the de facto underboss of one of the biggest criminal gangs north of the border.

He counted it as his right to be at the upper strata of the Scottish underworld. He had clawed his way up after living in his uncle's shadow for far too long. His uncle and his grandma had taken him in when he was a wee boy. His mother had been a useless alcoholic and occasional whore to whoever would buy her a vodka or two on a Saturday night. As a child, he had been slapped around and abused by his mother's "friends" for that night. He had heard her being fucked on the couch over and over again as he crouched in the dark bedroom, the bedcovers pulled over his ears to drown out the noise. He had been hungry and left alone more times than not and was left to wander the streets of Glasgow on his own. An urchin.

Then his uncle had stepped in and saved him. That night his mother disappeared and he never saw her again. Was she dead? Lost? He didn't know or care. He hated her. She was pathetic and weak. After that he had been raised into the family business and now it was in his blood. He knew he would be crowned the prince once his uncle passed on or retired, and Conor McLachlan had some big plans for his future empire. But in the meantime, he was free to run wild in the city, knowing he had the back up and "get out of jail free card" of his uncle and the rest of the crew.

He walked along the banks of the river until he came to the bridge that ran overhead. It was a place for druggies and winos to hide out of the rain, but not tonight. Tonight it provided the venue for a private meeting. A tall, stocky figure emerged; the copper in his usual heavy overcoat.

"So, what is this? Is it the Campbells trying to muscle in on our turf? They fuckin crazy. We'll hang them for this," barked McLachlan.

Detective Sergeant Willie Ollerton, of Glasgow Police's Criminal Investigation Division, shook his head and threw the remains of his cigarette in the water. "I don't know, Conor. Maybe. Perhaps they've decided they dinna want to play second fiddle to your uncle's operation anymore."

Conor looked down at the inky blackness of the river, his mind turning over the events of the night. "So, what do we know about the crew that took down McCoist's lads?"

Ollerton grimaced. "Oh, it wasn't a crew. Didn't I tell you that? According to the survivor of the shooting – before he lost consciousness –it was just one man."

"Fuck off!"

"It's what he said. One man. Business suit, dark sunglasses. Shotgun. The survivor said the accent was London."

"An outside gang?"

"Maybe the Campbells have brought in an outside contractor to do their dirty work for them?" reasoned Ollerton.

"What... a hitman?"

"It certainly looks that way. If they are ready to make a move on your operation, it makes sense to take out the hard men first."

"We need to hit them back. Fast," spat Conor, the venom clear in his voice.

Ollerton shrugged. This was way outside what he was paid for by the McLachlan gang. He was just a messenger, a conduit for information, someone to make a piece of evidence or body disappear off the official charts... and some unofficial ones too. "That's up to you, Conor. You're the man in charge while your uncle's away."

Conor McLachlan turned on him, his face pulled into a snarl. "Oh, don't think you've finished with this one, copper. You get yer arse in gear and find out what the fuck this is about!"

"But..."

"But me no buts. Get your contacts to work. Let's find out who's behind this. You find out who the hitter is. I'll deal with the Campbells. I'll have them swinging from the lampposts by their fucking necks before daylight."

Ollerton nodded. "Ok. I'll see what I can find out, but it might take a few hours. What about your uncle? Shouldn't you tell him?"

Conor shook his head. "I'll not have my uncle bothered until we have something more concrete. You leave my uncle to me. I'm in charge of the business while he's away. Now you, be on your way. Get your little police brain working. I want bodies and answers as soon as you can. I'll give ye a few hours to find out some information, but I want you and everybody from the crew back at the warehouse at midnight. No exceptions, understand?"

Ollerton had almost made it back to his front door when he was taken. He had driven straight home, needing to think. He parked the car in the next street, as was his habit. He was always careful of whom he was seen with. He was more scared of being caught with the known criminals who paid his wages than of chancers that might try to mug him. Some little scumbag trying to "mars bar" him was nothing, but being arrested for corruption was a place he didn't want to go.

He had taken his first "dip" when he was a fresh-faced policeman walking the beat around the tenements in the early 1960s. Five pound to look the "other way." After that he had upped his income when the McLachlans had taken over the Glasgow underworld, and he had made it up to detective. Over the past ten years it had been a mutually beneficial relationship.

The McLachlans had it all. They had murdered their way up to control all the vice, gambling and organised robbery in the city. The family had initially been under the control of old man McLachlan, Big Tommy, best known for massacring his foes with a meat cleaver. He had worked as an enforcer for the Krays in London in the 1960s, before he'd returned to Glasgow and started his own "firm." He had started small by opening a series of clubs and dance halls which were all fronts for his crime gang. But when he'd keeled over from a heart attack one day, his only son, Danny, had stepped up and taken over the gang.

Danny McLachlan had been the thinker, the planner, the strategist. He had gone from being the chubby kid forever in his old man's shadow, to running with the Glasgow street gangs, to being catapulted into the top spot as the heir apparent to Big Tommy's criminal empire. But young Danny had seen beyond protection money and armed robbery. He had visions of making his family even more influential with the organised crime gangs south of the border and to do that he needed to step into the ever growing and lucrative narcotics trade.

"Fat Danny" had come up with the novel idea of purchasing a fleet of ice-cream vans and having them travel around the housing estates selling their wares. In fact, the vans didn't just sell ice cream and sodas; the stuff under the counters was more profitable and highly illegal, namely heroin. He knew enough to start small, get the buyers hooked and then up the price. And it had worked. The McLachlan gang had a good run for the first two years with profits hitting the million mark. But in this trade, there was always the threat of competition and other gangs muscling in. The Finney gang, a small-time unit from the Gorbals, had begun the war. Threatening the van drivers and stealing the profits from the ice cream van tills and had soon escalated to shooting and punishment beatings. The McLachlans didn't take it sitting down, and on a humid night in August, Danny McLachlan organised his soldiers and hit the Finney gang in one brutal onslaught. By the time the night was over, all the leaders of the Finneys had been shot dead and the underbosses had either been run out of the city or "persuaded" to work for Fat Danny.

After that, Danny McLachlan's reign over the city had been complete. He controlled the heroin trade, was crime boss of all illegal activity in the region and he had been wise (and wealthy) enough to buy both judicial and police contacts that could get him and his family out of any serious trouble if the worst happened. So far, Danny McLachlan had never set a foot inside a prison cell, and most of that had been down to the influence and activities of his man within Glasgow CID, Detective Sergeant William Ollerton.

Ollerton now approached his house like he normally would, key in hand and ready to open the door, when he felt a strike to the side of his head, followed by a chop to the neck. Almost instantly, powerful arms had him in a choke hold and he felt his mouth being covered with one rough, calloused hand. The final indignity was his legs being swept out from under him. He crashed to the floor on his backside. A second shadowy figure emerged from the shadows. Ollerton had just enough time to see a small, thin man in a suit and a balaclava move off to his rear before he felt a sharp scratch to the side of his neck. Within seconds the powerful arms that controlled him relaxed and instead the chemical cocktail that had been injected began to take effect and Ollerton slipped away to unconsciousness.

Chapter Three

Torture is Torture

9.30 pm – East End of Glasgow

"Hold his head for me, Jojo. I don't want him flailing about. We don't need this to get any messier than it already is," said the strong, firm, no nonsense voice.

He hung upside down, his feet wrapped in a chain tied to a meat hook. His head dangled several feet off the floor and his hands were bound behind his back with his own handcuffs. Ollerton felt small, vice-like fingers grip both sides of his head, digging hard into his temple and his jaw. His eyes bleary, he assumed from being drugged, left his vision a wee bit out of focus. Then, suddenly, he felt himself being pulled backwards at an angle and listened to the scraping noise of the rollers above him as he was transported from one side of the freezing cold store room to the other. It was an abandoned abattoir in another part of the city, isolated and it was secured. DS Ollerton was going nowhere, he was sure. He had been involved with the McLachlan gang in things like this before. He knew how it worked.

The meat hook came to a rest directly underneath a rigged-up lamplight that bathed the man in a yellow glow. He became aware of two hidden figures moving about and organising things in the surrounding darkness. In his chest, he could feel his heart going at a terrific rate. He had been wrong before... THIS was far worse than being arrested for corruption. At least that way he might be able to talk his way out via his solicitor. No, this was far worse, because if he was right, these were the people who murdered a crew and razed a heroin stash to the ground in the space of a few hours. His senses began to return to him. His vision started to clear as did the numbness in his feet and fingers. As a test, he tensed his wrists and ankles to see how tight the restraints were. He strained but quickly came to the conclusion that it was futile. He and this meat hook were going to be together for a while yet.

Then, like actors on a stage, the dark shadows made their presence known. They both stepped in into his field of vision, and he saw them clearly for the first time, albeit upside down. Two men, one of below average height and fit-looking, in a dark business suit, the other smaller, whip like, his hair slicked back like a Teddy boy. He had taken his suit jacket off and was down to shirtsleeves. Both men regarded their captive for a while. Finally, the first man spoke.

"Ok, Jojo, you're up. Get ready for work."

The whip like man began to roll up his shirt sleeves, exposing the knotted muscles in his forearms. The other man, obviously the man in charge, momentarily went away and then returned with a wooden chair. He placed it a few feet away from Ollerton and turned it around so he was able to lean his forearms along the chair back. Ollerton thought he looked like a man settling himself in for a night watching the TV.

The man in charge removed a leather sharpening strop from his trouser pocket and then, as a follow up, took out and opened an old bone handled cut-throat razor. He flicked it open one handed and inspected the edge of the blade. He grunted, seemingly unhappy with what he saw. One end of the leather strop he hooked around the toe of his shoe and the other end held tight, stretched out in his fist. Then he slowly moved the blade of the razor up and down, up and down, honing the edge, his body moving in motion with the steel. And all this time his eyes never left the face of DS Willie Ollerton. Not once.

While all this was happening, Ollerton remained aware of the smaller, wiry man, off to the side. He had finished rolling up his sleeves and was now in the process of warming up his upper body in the manner of an amateur boxer about to go into the ring. He stretched out his arms and cracked the knuckles on both hands before working in a shadow boxing routine of jabs, uppercuts and hooks. Thirty seconds later he finished and began gently bouncing from foot to foot.

"You ready, Jojo?" asked the man in charge, still honing the razor.

"Sure am, boss," said the boxer.

"Then go to work."

The man known as Jojo sauntered up, his fists up ready for action, ready to do his job. Too late, DS Willie Ollerton realised what was about to happen and began to protest. "No… No… don't do it… plea…se." The fists landed perfectly and they landed hard straight into the ribs in a one two combination. The only thing that stopped the ribs from shattering on the first hit was that Ollerton had a good layer of body fat, built up by years of abuse, which took the brunt of it. The air rushed from his body and he doubled over in pain. Just as he doubled over, another shot landed on his kidneys, forcing him to jerk back up. This time he managed to find air from somewhere deep in his lungs and he let out a yelp of pain.

"Nice work, Jojo. You been training?"

"Little bit, boss. Like to keep my hand in when I can. You know me," said Jojo, working imaginary uppercuts into thin air.

Gorilla Grant continued with the smooth motion of the blade against the leather. He glanced casually over at the fat policeman, "I won't waste your time. I need information and I want it quick."

Ollerton regained his breath, calmed himself. "Do you know who I am... the amount of shite I can bring down on your head? This is my town. I'm a fucking police officer, you fucking cretin."

Still Gorilla made the blade move against the leather. "Jojo, a bit of respect here, I think."

Jojo moved in one fast motion, sending a crushing hook into the side of Ollerton's head and causing it to rock to the side. Ollerton saw stars and could feel the swelling start to rise on his busted-up eyelid.

Gorilla glared at his captive. "I know who you are. I know what you are. Bent copper, right? I could care less. It's easy as anything. You tell me what I want or we start hurting you for real."

"The McLachlans will hang you up by yer balls. So... Fuck off!"

Jojo looked over and Gorilla nodded. Jojo put another couple of shots into the ribs and watched as the upturned man sagged against his restraints.

"Where do the McLachlans meet up, if there's a big job going down and they need to rally the troops?" asked Gorilla.

"I...I dinna know, I swear to God," wheezed Ollerton.

"Oh of course you know. You just don't want to tell me."

Ollerton said nothing and glared back at his captors.

Gorilla nodded. "I'm impressed. I didn't think that you'd hold out this long. We were trying to work out which would give out first: your mouth or your heart. Maybe I've underestimated you. Still, never mind... you'll talk eventually."

"The brass, boss?" asked Jojo.

"The brass, Jojo, yes. Thank you."

Jojo went over to his suit jacket, which was draped over the back of a nearby chair, and rummaged in the inside pocket. When he turned around he was nursing a brass knuckle duster on his right hand. It looked used and well worn. He walked over and once more stood before the hanging man, studying him, picking his target on the body. Ollerton, seeing this immediately, tensed his body and his jaw – the guts and the face were the likely targets, he imagined. So he was shocked when Jojo shifted his weight and threw a devastating right cross straight into the centre of Ollerton's left shin, with a palpable sound of bone crunching. The Detective howled with pain and jerked like a fish on a hook.

"You ready to talk yet?" asked Gorilla calmly, but still there was nothing from the hanging man.

Another nod from Gorilla Grant. Jojo hit again and again, each strike producing a chilling crunch as bone shattered and flesh turned to pulp. Each time Ollerton screamed for his life and each time Gorilla's face remained passive while he continued to strop the razor back and forth.

"Want to know what we need?" asked Gorilla pleasantly.

A grunt, a gasp of breath. On the fourth or fifth time, Ollerton wasn't sure, the metal fist hit his fast-disintegrating bones, he gave way to unconsciousness.

"I'm glad you could join us," said the voice, a sense of menace in it.

He had come to in a daze; the rancid odour of smelling salts had jolted him back to the hell of reality. Had it been a dream? No, they were still there; the wiry man wielding the knuckle duster and the older man stropping the razor. The man in charge. The hit-man from the bar, Ollerton guessed.

"As I was saying, do you want to know what we need from you? Ok. I'll assume that you do. We want to know where the boyos go when the big chief calls them. Where do they meet up, where do they gather when the boss is planning a big job? Where is their safe house?" asked Gorilla.

Jojo landed another hit, this time near the knee. ""ARRGGHHH... ok... ok... ok... the warehouse!!"

"Which warehouse?"

"It's a place that they own, used to belong to a shipping company, down by the docks. It's registered to a front company so their name doesn't appear on the deeds. Folsom Shipping Logistics. The top floor is the office... the other few floors are for the lads to store their gear and to hide the stuff they've stolen. I can give you the address... he wants the crew, the rest of the muscle, everybody there at midnight," said Ollerton.

Gorilla nodded, pleased. "Thank you, detective, we'll find it. Alright, Jojo, you can put the knuckles away for the moment."

Ollerton, bloodied and battered, issued a sigh of relief.

"We'll get you fixed up soon and take you to the nearest hospital. Your story is that you got set upon by a gang of street rats. That way you'll be square with the police and the McLachlans, ok?" said Gorilla reassuringly.

Ollerton nodded. That seemed to be the most realistic chance for his own survival. He just hoped that CID and Fat Danny would buy it.

"There's just one more thing that we need you to do for us. Fat Danny's solicitor, that ponce Marcus Britten. He's holed up in his apartment with his boyfriend. We need you to get him out of there, so we can pick him up. I mean, it's not like he'll just let us into the building with open arms, is it?" laughed Gorilla to Jojo.

"I...I...I could do that. It wouldn't take much," said Ollerton.

"I know, Willie. I know you're the link man between Danny's criminal activities and the stuff the lawyer is involved in. All as thick as thieves, aren't you?"

Ollerton said nothing, but inside his mind was turning. How did this Englishman know the inside working of the McLachlan clan? How? The Campbells must have good spies.

"So here is what will happen," said Gorilla. "First, take a breath, get yourself calm. Then, in a moment, I'm going to bring over the telephone line we have rigged up here for our temporary home and you are going to make a very special phone call. Phone Britten and tell him Fat Danny himself has ordered that he make his way to his office straight away. Fat Danny will be waiting outside for him. He has something very, very important to discuss. Will that play, Willie?"

Ollerton agreed it would. If Danny McLachlan said jump, Marcus Britten QC would ask how high.

"Excellent! I don't need to warn you that any funny business, any secret codes, any sneaky beaky messages between you two and the consequences will be...violent. So violent, in fact, that they will spread to number 34 Morland Street. Do you understand what I mean?"

Ollerton understood alright. Morland Street was the home of his retired father. These killers would no doubt pay his father a visit and end his life... IF they were feeling generous. "I get it... I'll do what you need."

Ollerton craned his neck when Gorilla held the handset next to his head. He heard the whirr of the dial tone, the click as it was answered, then a pause before a weary voice spoke onto the line. Ollerton went at it, not giving the lawyer on the other end time to react. "Marcus, it's me, Ollerton. Get your shoes on. There's a meeting being called, and they need you to attend."

"What. Now? Hang on... I've just settled myself for the night..."

"Don't fucking argue, you queer. This is big! It's the big man himself who wants you, over at the warehouse. He's back from abroad. The shit's hit the fan and he wants you there!"

A pause from the other end and then, "Ok...I understand. I'll get ready. When?"

Ollerton looked over at Gorilla, who silently mouthed the words to him. "An hour's time. Leave your place in an hour's time. That should make it just right for you to get there."

"Ok. I understand," said Britten down the line.

Gorilla killed the line and put the phone back on the butchers table, where it had been sitting all night. He turned and crouched down next to Ollerton, smiling. "Excellent work, detective. I couldn't have done it better myself. And we think he'll definitely go, do we?

Ollerton nodded. "Oh aye. If he thinks Danny McLachlan is in town, he'd be there like a shot. Marcus is no fool, and a coward to boot."

Gorilla nodded, accepting the truth of the statement. "Yes, I think so too," he said. Gorilla knelt down so that he was beside the man's head and then, in one swift movement, he grabbed Ollerton's body with one hand to hold it steady, while with the other he moved the razor he had been honing for the past few moments across Ollerton's throat in a straight line. The cut was true and deep. There was the initial spray of blood that threw itself out onto the floor of the abattoir and then finally the flow slowed until it resembled an open tap. A look of surprise, horror and pain bloomed on Willie Ollerton's face as he hung upside down, swinging, blood from his arteries covering his face. Within moments it looked as though he wore a blood-red mask.

Gorilla Grant wiped the excess blood from the razor with an old rag, and both he and Jojo watched the policeman slowly die. When it was done, Gorilla turned to Jojo. "Be on your way. You have a good forty-five minutes to get in place."

Chapter Four

Jojo

10.45 pm – Jordanhill, Glasgow

Jojo McKay sat calmly in the darkness and watched the light in the window of the house of his target. He flexed his fingers and coiled them around the wooden toggles connected by the piano wire. It wasn't his chosen method of "offing" someone, but the boss had specific rules about what he wanted for this contract and Jojo, as Gorilla's man, was more than amenable to carrying them out.

Born and raised on the tough streets of Toxteth, Liverpool, Jojo McKay knew the language of violence intimately. The young Jojo had quickly fallen afoul of the local police. His reputation as a boxer, street fighter and troublemaking teenager grew fast. With his options limited, he had decided to make the Army his new career and had joined up with the Parachute Regiment. After basic training, he had risen to the rank of corporal during the crisis in Aden. He had killed his first terrorist on the streets of Mansour three months into his tour of duty. Four years later, and after "getting out," he had turned his hand to mercenary work. Bit in Africa, bit in Asia, bit everywhere, really. Then one night in Angola, he had killed a man in a bar fight, something about a late payment on a hand of cards, and had quickly fled the country. He had buggered about in Europe, staying out of the mercenary circles for a while, and had worked as a bouncer and leg breaker for several bar owners in Belgium. For what he lacked in height and build, he more than made up for in physical toughness and tenacity. There was many a "hard case" who quickly discovered that underestimating the physically unprepossessing Jojo was a serious mistake. They had the black eyes, broken nose and busted ribs to prove it. Jojo was that good with his fists.

A year later, Gorilla Grant had found a recently divorced and down on his luck Jojo propping up a bar in Kuala Lumpur. He had heard there was a British merc looking for a bit of part time security work and approached him. Jojo had weighed up the older, well-dressed man in front of him. He had noted the average-sized frame, solid build, and ready stance. Jojo had fought men bigger and bulkier than this fellow and won, but the face and the eyes gave him pause. They were set in a grim lock; eyes of contained fury and ready violence. Jojo knew instantly THIS was a man he would never be able to beat in any form of combat, for while Jojo was a street fighter and soldier, he recognised with an innate sense of survival that this was a man of shadows and stone-cold killer in a class of his own.

Their first job together had been essentially a snatch job for the Libyans. They had picked up a rogue arms dealer to find out what he knew. Jojo had been the surveillance man and driver on that job. After that it had become more regular all over Europe and the Middle East. The boss paid well and was a man to be respected, and Jojo was happy to serve as Gorilla Grant's squire as he was needed. Their relationship had stayed on a strictly professional basis. Mr Grant knew where to draw the line. He had his own private life that he kept sacred.

And then, six months ago, he had received a phone call from Mr Grant telling him he would be out of circulation for an extended period. "Don't try to look for me, Jojo, I'll find you when I'm done. It's a bit of personal business I have to attend to," said Grant.

"Look, boss, if it's something I can help with...."

Grant had closed him down, a sad tone to his voice. "There is nothing you can do to help in this case, Jojo. There is nothing anyone can do. But...thank you."

And that had been that. Jojo McKay had been cut loose from his regular employer and left to drift. He had returned home to visit family in Liverpool, had even taken on some "bouncer" work in the clubs and pubs, more as a way to keep busy than for the money. After the contracts he had been involved in with the "Gorilla," he was more than comfortably off. Then, just when he had given up hope, when he assumed he would never hear from Mr. Grant again, there he sat at the end of the bar in Matthew Street, where Jojo was working the doorman shift. He had smiled and walked over.

"Hello, boss. Good to see you."

"Evening, Jojo. Grab a seat. Thought we might have a little chat. I've a job coming up if you're interested. North of the Border. Something a bit special."

And that had been that. Gorilla Grant and Jojo McKay had been back in business. Except, once the planning had started, Jojo noted that the boss had changed... he was different somehow. A coldness had settled over this already hard man. There was a cruel tone to what he wanted to do during the contract. Perhaps even viciousness. The Gorilla had always had a propensity for violence, but now it seemed he wanted to gorge himself on the killing of these gangsters.

But Jojo held his counsel. He had worked with Gorilla Grant long enough to know not to overstep the mark or enquire into areas he wasn't invited. The boss never told him what had happened during the six months hiatus… but Jojo, in a moment of uncharacteristic empathy, sensed that Gorilla Grant had lost someone close to him. Occasionally the fury would fade from his eyes and be replaced by a sadness, perhaps even tears. Then, almost as quickly, the sadness would be wiped away to be once again be replaced by rage and violence. And what violence! The cutting of the dead copper's throat had been a case in point; it had been brutal and bloodthirsty. Jojo wasn't sure if it was to terrorise the rest of the targets or to quench Gorilla's bloodlust.

Jojo noticed that the upstairs light had gone off, replaced by the downstairs hallway light. There was a pause and then the shuffling figure of Marcus Britten, wrapped in a heavy overcoat, walked out onto his drive. Jojo had "bumped" the locks on the Rover. In truth, it had been an easy car to lock pick. A five-year-old could have done it. The manufacturers always put crap locks on vehicles these days. They might as well not bother, he thought. He heard the man heave himself into the driver's seat, grunt and then fumble, trying to get the keys in the ignition in the dark. The man sat upright again, and Jojo slowly rose and carefully snaked the wire over the head rest and the man's head… and then he pulled with all his strength. The man in the driver's seat bucked wildly, his hands instinctively coming up to his throat in the hope that he could get his fingers underneath the tension of the wire and be able to breathe.

Jojo pulled the wire tighter, the toggles of the garrotte firm in his leather gloved hands. He knew it wouldn't take long. The man was too unfit and out of shape and Jojo McKay was in a position of strength. Moments later he heard a gurgling noise and felt the body in front of him go slack. There was an aroma of blood in the air. The wire, inevitably, had cut through the flesh of the man's throat. In truth, Jojo had expected him to fight on for a bit longer. Probably his heart had given out, Jojo reasoned.

After that, Jojo simply left the wire around the man's neck for someone to find. The point wasn't just to murder; it was also to send a message. After all, nothing says "I can get to you anytime I want to" like the garrotted corpse of a stalwart of the legal profession. As a final move, Jojo removed a small piece of paper from his jacket pocket and pushed it into the mouth of the now immobile and very dead Marcus Britten, Queens Council and legal representative of Danny and Conor McLachlan. Jojo knew exactly what it said. Gorilla Grant had chosen it specifically. It was a page of the Bible, from the Old Testament. Hosea 9:9.

They have deeply corrupted themselves, as in the days of Gibeah: therefore he will remember their iniquity, he will visit their sins.

It was a tactical move, certainly, but also it showed that, in Jojo McKay's opinion, Mr. Grant still had a flair for the dramatic.

It was what made Gorilla Grant one of the best contract killers in Europe.

Chapter Five

A Night in the City

11.15pm – Cambulsang, Glasgow

Detective Inspector Bill McKilvaney sat in the squad car and sheltered from the rain. He watched as the emergency services, the fire brigade and the ambulance men, went about damping down the aftermath of the inferno. He knew the way it worked. After the razed building was declared structurally safe, the difficult job of recovering the charred bodies would begin.

Mckilvaney was a small, neat man who had earned his thirty years in the Glasgow Police force through good old-fashioned detective work and pragmatic acceptance of his lack of ambition. In truth, he had found the comfortable spot in his career and was happy to stay cosseted in it. The only thing that spoiled his life was the nefarious actions of the McLachlan crew.

But the chaos of tonight, well, he had never seen anything like it. Whoever it was, they were certainly mobile and professional enough that, so far, they hadn't been spotted. Hit and run tactics. Guerrilla style. Get in, attack, get out and then move onto the next target. First the shoot out in the bar, then the torching of a suspected McLachlan safe house, of which he was staring at the remains. And now, the latest piece of information was that Willie Ollerton, a Detective Sergeant from his own CID had been found, following an anonymous tip off, murdered. Strung up like a side of beef and with his throat cut.

On the surface, Glasgow was its normal self, but underneath McKilvaney, an old school policeman, knew something was badly amiss. He suspected the start of a gang war on his patch, something he definitely didn't want, not that he could do much about it at the minute. Information was coming in slowly, and it was sketchy at best, added to the fact that his department was underfunded, under resourced and under staffed. He knew the way it went. Nothing would get done until morning when Glasgow CID would start the mopping up process and try their best to discover who had been behind the night of chaos and anarchy. He was resigned to the fact that he and his men would probably never discover what had happened. He was sure, no he knew, that the McLachlan's had too many paid informants inside the police. They had the city sewn up tight and too many investigations from years gone by, everything from armed robbery and drug dealing to murder, had been scuppered due to their insidious influence.

The McLachlans had been the bane of his existence throughout most of his police career; first the father and then the son and now the nephew. He hated them all with a passion. Whatever and whoever was making trouble and causing them grief, he was more than willing to let them get on with it and complete the job. As long as no innocent civilians were killed or hurt in this war, he would be quite content, for one night, to stand on the wings and applaud the demise of the McLachlans. He turned his attention back to the crime scene. They were bringing the bodies out now.

Just a normal Saturday night in Glasgow, he thought.

12:15 am – Team safe house, Bearsden, outskirts of Glasgow

"You getting too old for this?" asked Maggie.

Gorilla shook his head. "I doubt it," he said. "I just thought it best to take a pause before the rest of the night plays out.

They sat in the control room of the operations base for this contract, which in reality was the kitchen of the safe house they had appropriated for the night. They had completed checks several days ago, and discovered the owners were going away for the weekend, to a wedding in Aberdeen. Then they had simply sprung the locks and let themselves in earlier that day. It was warm, safe and unnoticed. By the early hours of the morning, they would leave the house and it would be as if they had never been there.

Gorilla Grant sat at the kitchen table, his suit jacket draped over his chair, his tie loosened, the buttons of his waistcoat undone and his shirt sleeves rolled up. The pump action shotgun lay broken into sections before him and an oiling rag was in his hand. He had several rows of shotgun rounds lined up in front of him that he would chamber once he'd finished the routine of cleaning and oiling. A stack of sandwiches and several mugs of hot sweet tea sat waiting at the opposite side of the table, sustenance for later. At the kitchen sink, Jojo McKay bathed his hands in cold water, trying to alleviate the welts and pain from the last hit, the strangulation, on the legal eagle.

Maggie Hart stood leaning against the sink, her hands folded across her chest and a look of concern on her face. A good-looking blonde in her early forties, she wore jeans and a jumper to keep the cold out. Gorilla and Maggie went back, they had history. They had met years ago during a job they were both involved in. When the operation had ended they had gone their separate ways but had had stayed friends and in touch on a professional basis. She had been one of the best undercover operators in the British Army. Maggie had worked against the IRA in Belfast, often operating solo in hard-line provo areas with only a Browning 9mm and her quick wits keeping her alive. Once she had left the military she had decided to work as a freelance intelligence operative, which is when she came to the attention of Gorilla Grant. For this contract, she was responsible for managing the safe house and getting everything out once they had finished. She was thorough and professional. Maggie was in a class all of her own.

"You should have stayed out," she said. "You'd been through enough, lost enough over the past few months. Someone else could have picked this up."

"I had to. I needed to do this. It helps me," said Gorilla.

"What? Keeps your mind busy? I get that."

He shook his head, telling her that her analysis wasn't correct and he didn't want to delve too deeply into this aspect of the conversation. In his dark 3am moments, Gorilla Grant would admit to himself that the main reason that he had taken this contract was to purge the fury and violence inside him. It was like a cancer, had been for the past six months. He could feel it rising… his red mist. He was a professional. A professional spy, intelligence operator and contract killer, and if he wanted to stay doing what he did best, he recognised he would have to exorcise this rage. To him, what better way than to eliminate a clan of murderers and gangsters? It was killing two birds with one stone really. Once that rage had subsided, he was sure, he would at least be able to grieve and to heal in peace.

"She wouldn't have wanted you to be like this," said Maggie bluntly.

"You didn't know her. How would you know what she would have wanted?"

"Because I know me, and she sounds a lot like me. I don't want you to be like this; cold, vicious, it's not you, Jack."

"Just leave it, Maggie. Please."

She nodded, accepted that she had gone as far as she could go with her point and changed the subject. "So, what's next?"

"We do an ammo check. We hit the road to get down to the warehouse by midnight. When it's all over and the contract is complete, I phone here, the usual wrong number call, and you pack up and shift out. We rendezvous in Birmingham at the Central Hotel. After that, I contact the client and confirm that the contract has been completed. We get our money and we all go home," said Gorilla, reassembling the shotgun.

Maggie nodded. She was starting a different job next week, for a different contractor, so it was all money to her. But still, it didn't stop her being concerned for Jack Grant. It was what Gorilla Grant and people of his ilk were good at: getting in close to the target. Hit and run guerrilla raids at dead of night, being ruthless when it was time to pull the trigger. But all this bloodlust, all this murder. It just wasn't up to Gorilla's usual code. It somehow didn't sit right with her. She didn't know who the client was on this contract, but she assumed it was a rival gang that wanted to off the opposition. That shocked her: Gorilla Grant, with his international reputation, was resorting to working for lowlife scum.

It was a strange setup, and one that Gorilla seemed to be enjoying, but she supposed when you lost the love of your life like he had recently, you would do anything to take the pain away.

Chapter Six

The Gathering of the Clan

1.30 am - Penthouse Apartment, Folsom Shipping Warehouse, James Watt Street, Glasgow

Conor McLachlan, surrounded by his men, felt like a young Roman general ready to vanquish his enemies from the gates of Rome. He stood behind his uncle's desk and stared at the hard faces that made up the rest of the McLachlan clan, twelve of them in total. Some were cousins who had been brought in from the outer cities, others were sub-lieutenants who had worked their way up, and many were gang members responsible for all the drug dealing, extortion, robbery and violence on behalf of the McLachlan family in Glasgow.

"We think the Campbells are trying to wipe out my uncle's organisation tonight. You already know what happened to Billy McCoist and his boys, what happened to the drug stash. Well.... I want it stopped now. So, we took a hit earlier this evening. We were on the back foot. Well, lads, WE are going to turn this thing around. No gobshite Campbells are taking what's ours. I have a list of addresses of Campbell businesses and family members.

I want them all cowering or dead by morning. Is that understood?"

There was a mutual mumbling of acceptance and the odd "Aye, Conor." They were all career criminals, men who had done prison time, men who considered casual violence a way of life. They were armed with everything from pickaxe handles to butchers' knives to pistols and sawn-off shotguns. They were the best that could be mustered at short notice and they knew it.

"Now," continued Conor, "these cunts have hired in an outsider, a hit man, to do their dirty work, not man enough to do it themselves. So far this hit man has had it all his own way. We know what he looks like and what he's armed with. Me and the twins are gonna take care of him. Davy, Frank, Archie, you hang here for a while, in case we need backup. I want the rest of you to hit the Campbells."

The men gripped their array of weapons tighter in their fists. No one was going to take away the money they had earned at the hands of the McLachlans. They would kill for that.

"Move out, boys," ordered Conor. "Take no prisoners. No fucking surrender."

Jojo had been in place for the past fifteen minutes. He had a good spot hidden inside an abandoned shed some thirty feet away from the main doorway of the warehouse. He knew the boss was in a similar hide further down the quayside, but where Mr Grant had his trusty pump action shotgun ready, Jojo had something far louder. In a canvas rucksack in front of him he had access to ten fragmentation grenades.

The grenades –British Army L2-A2 Anti-Personnel Fragmentation Grenades they had "acquired" from a mercenary contact of Jojo's in London –were filled with a composition B explosive and had a 4.4 second fuse from the moment the pin was removed. For close quarter engagements, they were the perfect weapon to take out a small team of enemy soldiers, so against a group of unprepared criminals it would be a turkey shoot.

He saw three men move out of the front entrance and slam the door behind them. He knew this was it. Gorilla had given strict instructions that no one was to leave the warehouse alive. He picked up the first grenade and pulled the pin, igniting the fuse. Jojo knew if he hit it right, one grenade should take out the hard men in one fell swoop. He threw it overhand and watched as it arced, the reflection from the orange streetlight giving it the aura of a ball of fire travelling at speed. It landed three feet in front of the men who had emerged from the warehouse.

"One...two...three....," counted Jojo.

The boom blasted apart the silence of the night and shattered the bodies of the gangsters in its wake. Jojo had just a moment to register them being lifted up, and then bodies and limbs flew in several directions at once, but for Jojo, one wasn't enough. No sooner had the first one detonated then he had pulled the pins on two more and threw them, one after another, at the same targets. He could hear the screaming of the survivors from across the road, and then the two grenades landed and exploded.

There was no more wailing. A final glance at the kill zone confirmed that nothing moved there.

From the shadows further down the quayside, the figure of the shotgun-wielding Gorilla Grant emerged. The shadow ran at speed, the weapon held out in front of him in case an unexpected target appeared, and he easily circumvented the slaughter. Without breaking stride, he kicked in the main entrance door to the warehouse that the grenades had virtually demolished.

Jojo saw Gorilla Grant disappear inside and checked his watch. 12:30am. He knew Gorilla would sweep through the warehouse hunting targets in minutes. He was that good. Jojo also knew it wouldn't take long before the law would be roused, and that he'd better organise the escape plan fast. He needed to fire up the beast, the Jaguar.

.... In the now darkened corridor, Davey Sutton was being haunted by shadows. He had heard the explosions from outside and watched as the door exploded inwards. He himself had turned tail and run back down the corridor and into the heart of the warehouse. He stood at the corner, waiting for a target, and there was the figure, small and dapper, toting a big shotgun and heading straight for him. Davey was armed only with an iron crowbar, good for taking headshots, but not so good for attacking a devil with a pump action.

The hit-man, or whatever the fuck he was, saw Davey peeking out from the corner and fired. He aimed low, hitting Davey in the thigh. A scream and then he lay on the floor, a massive hole in his leg. The second blast took him square in the chest. The last thing Davey saw was the killer's shoes walking past him and heading up the stairs to the upper floors....

.... Archie Strong came rushing when he heard the noise of the shotgun blasts downstairs. He stood at the top of the stairs. Ready and waiting. It was he, an ex-army man, who had done his military service in the Middle East with the Desert Rats, who had come up with the idea of having a guard on each floor of the warehouse, just in case there was an attack. And he was right, had been born out in his assessment, because it was fucking happening now! Of course, what they really needed was McCoist's crew. They were the hard cases; they were the ones who had been in the army. But McCoist and his men had been gunned down earlier tonight by the very hit-man stalking them all now!

But Archie had learned a thing or two in the army, apart from spending the odd month in prison. He knew that the man with the higher ground always has the tactical advantage. The problem was, he only had a machete. How the fuck was he meant to take down a psycho with a shotgun using a machete?

As he pondered this tactical conundrum, he felt his legs crumple. He didn't even hear the shotgun. All he saw was a bright flash from the darkness below, and then he couldn't hold his body upright anymore. He screamed as he looked down at his mangled knees. Then he saw the figure in the business suit coming up the steps towards him.

"Ye bastard!!!" was all that Archie could manage, that and a half-hearted slash with the machete. Gorilla simply finished him off with a fatal blast to the chest. He stepped over the dying man and made his way ever upwards.

At the top of the landing, Frank Dugan had already pissed himself while waiting for the elevator. He was that scared. He could feel it cold and damp against his trouser leg. In his hand, he held a small revolver with the standard six shots. He had never fired a gun in his life. That wasn't his speciality, wasn't what he did for the McLachlans. He was a pimp. He ran the whores. He was okay at slapping the tarts around, but could he shoot, and kill, whatever it was that was coming up that elevator? He honestly didn't know. And he wouldn't find out.

Behind him, a kick flung open the door to the emergency staircase and a shotgun blast took Frank Dugan in the chest, flinging him against the wall in a smear of blood. The second shot to the head killed him.

Gorilla Grant moved like a wraith through the darkened warehouse. The only sound he made was the inevitable clack-clack when he put another round into the pump action shotgun. So far, he had taken down eight of the McLachlan crew. He knew only the young prince and his bodyguards remained. Gorilla didn't foresee any problems there. This was nothing to him. It was no contest, really; several unfit, untrained and past their best criminals versus one of the best international gunmen in Europe, if not the world? It was like shooting fish in a barrel.

To a witness, Gorilla looked calm, as though going through a tactical routine. Aiming, firing on target, watching the target die, reloading. Fire and move, fire and move. The shotgun bucked against his shoulder with each round fired. All the necessary drills of close quarter battle controlled his movements as he proceeded through the warehouse and up the staircase, eliminating available targets. On the outside, he resembled a cold machine, but on the inside, he was a mask of red mist and blood rage. He needed an infinite number of bullets and an infinite number of targets to extinguish the rage from inside him. He needed to eliminate the pain, the grief, the loss the fury.

He counted down the men that he killed: one... two... three... four... five... six... seven... eight...

He made it onto the top floor of the landing, walked past the elevator and turned a corner into where he assumed the office space would be. Two large, hard-looking men stood outside the door to the office, each holding sawn off shotguns. The bodyguards, he guessed. They did alright, they reacted well. They saw him, managed to bring up the sawn offs and fire a blast each. The shot peppered the wall, missing Gorilla completely.

Amateurs, he thought. Crap ammunition and a moving target outside of the sawn off's range were not a good combination.

Another volley from the sawn offs, another impact on the wall providing him with cover. They were awful shooters.

Then there was a pause. He heard them trying to reload. Moving fast around the corner, he brought the pump action up smoothly and fired off rounds in quick succession. The first two took the big bald-headed bodyguard down. Chest and then head equals dead. Next, Gorilla switched his trajectory. Really, at fifteen feet, it was a no miss situation, and he aligned the sights on bodyguard number two. The man was fumbling trying to push a round into the sawn off. He looked up and realised he was out of time and shouted out, "No….NO…NOOO!!!!" as Gorilla's blasts took him out with several head shots.

Gorilla by passed the dead men and blasted out the lock to the penthouse apartment. A kick of the door and he was inside, searching the room for targets. The apartment was stylishly furnished in the manner of a playboy: soft lights, rugs, leather couches. Gorilla guessed it was used as an office/fuck pad for the top men. He pushed several more shotgun cartridges into the feeder tube, his eyes never leaving the room, still hunting, still searching. Then he thought he heard a noise from what he assumed was the bedroom. He went in fast and low, a kick to the door and drop to one knee, his back against the doorframe and the shotgun up and searching for targets. He scanned and took in a water bed, a mirrored wardrobe and a dressing table. Nothing else. It was empty. The noise had come from the open window and the blinds that had been left hanging at an awkward angle.

Conor McLachlan had escaped out of the window and down the rear exterior staircase.

Chapter Seven

The Bridge

Conor scrambled down the wet and slippery emergency fire escape as fast as his legs would carry him. The moment he had heard the explosions and the shooting he knew his plan to kill the Campbells that night was done for. His only option now was to run and regroup at a later date. Let his uncle try and sort this shite out. All he knew was that he had to get to his motor and get out of the city as fast as possible. He made it to the ground floor, still hearing the shotgun BOOMS and the screams of dying men in the distance, and ran to the car park at the side of the building. He made it to his car, an orange Ford Capri, fumbled for his keys and, once in the driver's seat, he pumped the accelerator of the Capri and spun it around and out of the parking. The tires squealed and speed soon replaced the burning of rubber as the car gained traction on the road.

Conor's only thought was to put as much distance as he could between himself and the… whoever the fuck it was that had taken out most of his crew. The Ford had a souped-up engine that one of the garages the family owned had fixed for him. It was possibly the fastest car in the city.

Where? Where could he run to? Most of the crew were dead or dying! He was sure there was no safe haven in Glasgow anymore. This fucking hit man seemed to know everything. He shifted the gears and increased the speed. The road in front of him had become a vignette of black with a solid white line hurtling towards him at speed. Think… think!

North. He could go North. No one would find him there. Lay low for a while. Wait it out until he could make contact with his uncle. Yeah… Danny McLachlan would sort it out. He would smash those fucking Campbells and their gobshite hit man into the ground. Yeah…that's what he'd do. He had a plan. He took the road out of Glasgow that would lead him North into the wilds and the mountains.

And then he heard the growl and saw the headlights of the black Jaguar in his rear-view mirror and he knew he would never see another mountain in his life.

Jojo McKay knew the Capri was fast, but in reality, nothing was going to outrun this beast of a Jaguar. Not this night. It was a done deal.

"Get him, Jojo," barked Gorilla Grant from the backseat. He was loading rounds into the pump action from an ammunition box in the rear foot well. Jojo noted that the boss looked calm and in control. A true professional. It was a pleasure to work for him. Jojo put his foot down to the floor and the Jaguar sped up so its nose was ahead of the Capri. He risked a glance sideways and saw the tense, scared face of a young, redheaded man desperately trying to pump the accelerator of his car to out speed the Jaguar. No chance, sunshine, thought Jojo.

"Hold it steady, Jojo. One shot will finish this off," said Gorilla as he chambered a solid shot round. He wound down the window and poked the barrel of the shotgun out, aiming at the engine block of the other car. He steadied himself against the frame of the window and then fired. Against the roar of the engines, the boom of the shotgun was lost.

Gorilla knew what a solid shotgun round could do to an engine block of a vehicle. Whatever the shotgun round had hit caused the Capri to lurch rapidly and lose power quickly. For good measure, Jojo nudged the off side of the Jaguar against the right rear of the Capri, sending the already disabled car into a violent tailspin. The Capri spun once, twice, and then, on the third spin it upended in a corkscrew motion. It landed on its roof and skidded twenty feet until a nearby streetlight stopped it. By contrast, the Jaguar hit top speed as it overshot the crash site. Jojo slammed on the breaks and steered into the skid, bringing it to a controlled stop a further sixty feet away.

"You ok, boss?" asked Jojo, his heart racing like a jackhammer.

"Fine," murmured Gorilla calmly as he craned his neck to look out of the rear windscreen and back at the overturned car. Its front was mangled, the roof had caved in, the wheels spun wildly and smoke poured out of the engine block. But was Conor McLachlan dead inside? Gorilla took no chances. Instantly he leaped out of the back seat and ran towards the wreckage. He led with the shotgun up and ready to fire, but as he got closer, he could see there was no dead body inside, no mangled corpse. It was empty. What he could see, however, was a trail of blood that led away from the crashed car and into the wooded copse.

Conor ran like the devil was on his heels. He had lost his gun somewhere. His shattered left leg trailed behind him. That fucker, whoever he was... Christ, it had been a hell of a shot to take out his car like that. The crash had upended him and upon impact he had felt something snap in his leg. Through sheer terror he had managed to drag himself out of the vehicle. His breath rasped heavily, sucking in air, but he had to move, put distance there... anything to get him away from the demon with the shotgun. Those fucking Campbells and their bastard hit man from London.

He had been on a rural road on the outskirts of the city when he had crashed. His only escape route was to make straight for the woods. If he could not lose them completely, he could at least hide. He tripped twice, hauled himself back up and made his way through the brambles and the undergrowth. He prayed the darkness would be his friend and hide him. In the distance, he could hear the odd rumble of an early morning lorry or a truck. The motorway? It must be not far from the motorway. Maybe he could hijack a lorry and get the driver to take him somewhere... anywhere. He carried on for a few moments more and then he saw up ahead... It was a bridge, a foot pass really, that took walkers across from one side of the motorway to the other. If he could get across, he could be free. He was sweating now. He knew he was losing blood fast and there was the risk of going into shock. He made it half way across the bridge when his good leg gave out. He dropped to the floor, exhausted. It had been a long and painful night. His whole world, his whole future empire, brought crashing to the ground by this killer who hunted him. His crew gunned down, his drugs burned, his copper dead, the ambush that he had planned gone to shit. Fuck! He lay back on the cold wet asphalt of the road and stared up at the black night sky.

Then, clearly, with no subterfuge, he heard the sound of shoes marching at a steady pace towards him from the far side of the bridge. The streetlight shone behind the figure, giving it a mysterious and ominous silhouette. Once again it was small, fit, well-dressed and carrying that fearsome shotgun that kept spitting out death. Conor raised his head off the ground and watched as the killer approached. Fifty feet… thirty… a racking of the pump action shotgun… ten, until he was stood over him.

"Get on your knees. Do it now. I will help you if you can't manage it," snarled Gorilla.

Conor McLachlan, once Prince of the most powerful crime family in Scotland, knelt, defeated before Gorilla Grant. His sobs came in huge racking gulps. "Alright mister… alright… look we dinna have to do this. You could just let me go… tell the Campbells I will talk to my uncle for them. They can work out a deal… a good deal. They can have the whores… the coke…. the gambling. I have money… lots of it. You can have it. Just let me go. Tell the Campbells that you could ne find me. I'll just disappear… I'll never come back. I promise… oh please… I promise. Please!!"

Gorilla Grant cocked his head in a quizzical manner and frowned. When he spoke, it was clearly but with a note of genuine confusion. "Who are the Campbells? I don't know who you mean."

Connor's mind raced like a computer as he tried to figure out what was happening. His eyes twirled like whirly-gigs. Words failed. "Wha…? Yeh… wha…? Malachy and Robert Campbell. From Edinburgh……second rate shite gangsters…. yer employer!"

Gorilla Grant shook his head as he checked the safety was off the shotgun. "Not my employer's old son. Nothing to do with me, I'm afraid."

"Then what have we… what have I done to you?"

Gorilla shrugged. "You've done nothing to me. I don't even know who you are. It's nothing personal. It's just a job."

Conor McLachlan stared back, his mind blank. At last, Gorilla Grant put him out of his misery. "It was about the girl from years ago," he said. "Her name was Hannah. Her family paid for all of this. For me it's just a job... mostly."

For a few more moments, black confusion swirled in Conor's mind. Then, slowly, realization dawned. THAT girl. Suddenly his thoughts flared in a kaleidoscope of images he remembered from what... years ago? A girl in a bar, good looking, young, like he liked them. She had turned him down. Then the inevitable rage... the snatching off the street on her way home from the pub... holding her... having his fun with her... her screams... going too far... blood... disposing of the body. Then the inevitable police investigation his uncle had scuppered with the help of DS Ollerton. He thought he had gotten away with all that. Conor looked up at his executioner one last time and saw him place the open-ended barrel of the shotgun against his forehead.

Gorilla had a special round ready for the execution, a hard lump of metal he knew would obliterate the head of Conor McLachlan, Prince of the Glasgow underworld and Gorilla Grant's ultimate target for this particular contract.

It was over in a second, the pulling of the trigger and the execution of a criminal, rapist and murderer. Gorilla watched as the body slumped to the ground, its head cleaved completely in two down the centreline. It was just a mangled lump of meat. Gorilla felt nothing for the dead man, but what he did feel, like an epiphany, was a sudden calm, tranquillity, almost like a fire had been extinguished somewhere deep inside him. Gorilla turned and walked back through the wooded copse, and as he approached the road he heard a squeal of tyres as Jojo pulled up in the black panther of a Jaguar that was his escape vehicle. "It done, boss?" asked Jojo, the tension in his voice clear. He was eager to get out of this bloody city and be done with this contract. It had been a hell of a night.

Gorilla Grant nodded as he climbed into the car. "It's all done, Jojo. Let's move."

Happily, Jojo gunned the engine and drove off.

Soon the Jaguar would be dumped, set alight and they would then transfer over to a "clean" vehicle before heading south to cross the border into England. Not that the contract was completely finished, but Jojo didn't need to know about that. Within forty-eight hours Gorilla Grant would be travelling on a false passport and flying out of London Airport to find his final target.

Chapter Eight

Hannah

Glasgow, 1979

"My name is Hannah. Hannah Connolly. I am 23 years old. I am studying to be a Doctor at Glasgow University. But that is my past life. NOW I am scared. I can no longer breathe. I know that I am about to die soon. I am 23 years old...

I can see the face of my killer above me. It is an angry face, red haired, flushed and full of hate. The face scares me, but I can do nothing about that. He has his hands around my throat, has done for the past few minutes, I can feel... literally FEEL... the life ebbing away from me. I just want my mum... I want my mum... want to tell her how much I love her and how much I will miss her. I will never get to see her again, and that scares me more than the pain.

Mum always said that I was a good girl. Mum always called me beautiful. Brown haired and blue eyed and petite. Mum always called me her clever girl. Ever since my father passed away mum and I have become so, so close. She is my best friend and the one person who lifts me up when I'm down or defeated.

All I remember before the beating was walking home after the disco at the club, back to my student flat, then being grabbed and punched and thrown into a van of some kind. It was dark in the back of the van. I could smell sweat and disinfectant. I could hear male voices laughing up front in the driver's cab. We drove for how long? I don't know. Minutes or hours? It was all a blur... then the rear doors of the van opened up, briefly letting in the glare of a streetlight and the tall figure of HIM, my future killer. He spoke to me only once. "Hey, lassie, why did you have to be such a stuck up little cunt."

Then came more punches, the ripping of my clothes, my underwear, the molestation of my body......I fought back, scratched him hard across the face, drew blood, wounded HIM. That got me harder punches. I know now that I will never feel love, never be married, never be a mother to sons and daughters. My virginity was taken from me, by force, moments before. It was painful and I was scared, but mercifully it was quick. Just pain and the flow of HIM and the flow of my blood combined.

I remembered HIM. At first, I didn't believe that was who it was... the man from the club I had been at with my friends. He had tried to chat me up... offered to buy me a drink. I hadn't been interested, he wasn't my type really. Then, when I said no, he tried to put his hand up my skirt. I reacted without even thinking and slapped him, hard, once across the face. My friends had laughed at him. I had seen his reaction. One of shock, and then disbelief and then fury, pent up, barely held in check. He had turned and stormed from the club, pushing the doormen out of the way. The bouncers had been visibly scared of him, had parted like the Red Sea. Why would doormen, bouncers, do that? Who is HE?

And now, here, comes the blow that they were one and the same person. How scary is that? HE had the means and the will to molest a girl one moment then kidnap and rape her the next moment. Then the engine of the van starts again and brings me back to the last few moments of my life. The driver moves us around the city as I am trapped in the back with my killer, who stares at me with contempt. The van stops, the door opens and HE grabs me and throws me out of the van and onto the pathway. I scream in my mind as my killer pulls me by my hair, drags me along the path. I can't scream anymore. The beating he gave me has virtually broken my jaw and the choking has bruised my throat. The most I can manage is a weak mew. I know no one is coming to help me. I know HE will kill me soon.

I can hear the lap of water, from the river I would guess, and I know it will be my grave.

Then he stands over me, looking down at me as I lie half naked, pity and disgust slashed across his face. I am conscious enough to notice the half a house brick gripped in his right hand. In that moment, I know how the last moment of my life will end. HE kneels and places his left hand on my chest. His right hand raises the brick above his shoulder and takes aim. I can see the rough, jagged edge of the brick. My medical training tells me what kind of lethal trauma that can inflict upon a human skull. On my human skull.

I say a silent prayer to God, to protect my mum, my friends, my family. I just hope someone remembers me, spares me a thought on my birthday. I hope... I will miss my life. I feel so cheated that I never got to live any more of it. It is down to HIM that I feel this way... this spoilt child who hurts and rapes and snuffs out life at a whim.

I take one last look and see the hand with the brick in it as it comes hurtling down towards my head. In that split second, I feel the crunch, the blinding white light of pain and then...

I die.

LONDON, 1980

On the day she had walked away from identifying her younger sister's body, Lady Joanna Munroe, wife of the eminent member of the House of Lords, Lord Munroe of Argyle, made the decision to become a killer. It had been that clear in her mind. Not that she would be the one to pull the trigger or wield a knife –she was far too weak physically for that –but she would use her not inconsiderable resources to find the man who could.

She had held up her sister, her beautiful younger sister, at the funeral because poor Cassie had been a mess, understandably so. The death of Cassie's daughter Hannah, had destroyed her. Cassie had lost her husband to cancer last year and now her beautiful daughter. It had all been too much. Following the funeral, information had come from Glasgow Police that they had a suspect. A local criminal, they said. Joanna and Cassie had been buoyed by the news. Maybe this would help alleviate the pain. They had travelled up to Scotland following the funeral, eager to see what information the murder squad detectives had found.

Then the earth-shattering news came –they had to release the suspect. Witnesses had retracted their statements, a piece of evidence was tainted, another had been accidently lost or destroyed. With not much to go on, the Crown Prosecution Service hadn't had any choice but to close the case down. The lead detective, DCI Mckilvaney, had said to them through barely contained rage. "Ladies, we had to let that little bugger go. I know he did it, I know who he is and his family's reputation. He's a bastard… excuse my French, but with no witnesses and no evidence, it's a dead loss. They are officially shelving the case. I mean, the little bugger was even given an alibi!"

A shelved murder case. An injustice to a victim. A family traumatised. Three days later Joanna Munroe's sister hung herself.

Following the second funeral that year for her, Joanna Munroe started to plan. Planning was something she had a talent for, both the bigger picture and the fine detail. It was what had made her one of the most accomplished Intelligence officers of her time when she was operational for the Secret Intelligence Service. She had been a child of the Service. Her grandfather had done heroic things in Russia against the Bolsheviks, her father something similar against the Germans, so for her it was natural that she should be born into the world of espionage. She had been one of the few female operatives during the Cold War that had been on the front line. Of course, that had been a decade before, before she had retired and married Albion Munroe, aristocrat and Lord of the Realm. But back in her heyday she had operated against the KGB, sent agents across barbed wire fences to almost certain death. All her skills and experiences as a spy would be needed if she was to successfully complete what she had in mind.

She had already been given the name of her target –Conor McLachlan –unofficially by the detective investigating the case. Then she turned her focused eye on finding out everything about him, his family and his underworld connections. Joanna Munroe had spent years sifting through classified documents and looking for patterns in random events as a Desk Officer of SIS. After months of painstaking research, she felt ready to make her next move. She had a plan, she had the background to the target, now she needed people on the ground to discover as much up to date intelligence as possible. In her old employment, she would have called it "winding the clock."

The Secret Intelligence Service and its sister organisation, the Security Service has a long tradition of ex-employees going freelance in the private investigation and security business. It is a closed and secretive world, but for an insider who has worked beside these people as part of government service, it is a huge resource. Over the course of several months, Joanna Munroe gave orders for a diverse group of people to enter in and out of Glasgow. Some were there to make discreet inquiries, some were there to watch and observe, and others were there to call in favours from former colleagues in the police or military. All were discreet and left no trace of their activities. It had been a costly part of the plan, but worth it, and by the end of it all she had the most accurate and up to date information about her targets. She felt she knew them as well as any police intelligence unit ever could. She had their names, their ranks within the underworld, their locations, and their businesses. With the intelligence plan in place now she needed her soldier; the man that could lead her war.

Once again, she had made discreet inquiries among her former colleagues. At first, there had been nothing, and really, she had expected nothing. Slipping back into her old ways of being a spy had come naturally. Then, sooner rather than later, an old friend had mentioned a contact who might be able to help. The contact may know someone...maybe...possibly. It was worth at least checking out.

A luncheon at a certain private club in Knightsbridge, one for former members of the secret trade, was arranged. She had climbed the steps to the club's first floor dining room and waited patiently for her guest to arrive. She had listened to the discreet, muffled voices of the men and women dining around her. Listened to the talk of secret operations past and gone: Malaya, Aden, the paddies in Ireland, codenames, regiments......all talk from her past life. All gone now.

The man who approached her, his hand extended for the customary shake, was of medium height and dapper, his thinning hair definitely on the wrong side of grey, but his smile warm and welcoming. The man's name was Fergus, Fergus Penn, he said. He handed her his business card, emblazoned in gold print with the words Castle Security Services/Fergus Penn – Security Consultant. "Now what seems to be the problem that I can help you with?" asked Penn.

So she had told him. No tears, no hysterics, no emotion. She had kept it cool and calm, a business meeting, nothing more.

She had told him of Hannah, her death, of the court case that had collapsed because of missing evidence. Told him of her own investigation into what had happened. She had told him what she wanted.

Fergus Penn, former Captain in the Intelligence Corp and now highly paid security consultant to the rich and famous, had listened politely, placed down his knife and fork, dabbed at the corners of his mouth with the linen napkin, and then thanked his hostess for a wonderful lunch. He had stood, said he hoped she would forgive him but that he had a pressing appointment that had slipped his mind. He was so sorry, but if something came to light that he thought could help her, he would be in touch directly.

She had watched as he had turned and descended the stairs and out of the club. She had blown it! She knew by his reaction. She had made a mess of her pitch. The man would think she was an imbecile, either that or a deranged fantasist.

A week later she received a call. "I think I've found what you're looking for," said Penn. "I've booked a suite at the Plaza Hotel. I thought we could all get together and have a chat."

Two days later she made her way discreetly to the suite on the fifth floor. A gentle knock and Penn, the middleman, ushered her in. "This is Mr. Smith," said Fergus Penn. "Mr Smith is someone I have worked with previously. He is a man of his word and is to be trusted."

She appraised the man in front of her. He was in his fifties, of below average height, not tall and not short, with neatly-clipped grey hair, good shoulders and wearing a well-cut suit with a regimental tie. He looked like a cross between a sergeant major and a self-made businessman. His face was handsome but with a hard edge to it, she thought, but it was the eyes concealed behind his glasses that held her, grey blue and intense. She started her pitch like she would have in the old days with her agents.

"I understand that you are a man who has some experience with what I'm after," she said.

"I have experience in lots of things, but I'll be honest with you; I haven't worked for nearly a year. I may not be what you are looking for."

She ignored the remark. "Not worked through lack of opportunity?"

He shook his head. "Through choice."

"Then would you consider coming out of retirement? For me?"

He pondered. He shrugged. "Tell me about the job. Leave nothing out. I'll be honest; I have made enough money over the past few years to be able to retire comfortably, so it would have to be for a very good reason if I was to consider working again."

So she told him everything. Of her life, how she had worked behind the Iron Curtain spying against the Kremlin for his old service, of her beautiful niece, her beloved sister, the murder, the funeral, the travesty of a criminal investigation, her sisters suicide, her obsession with finding the killer, her plan for revenge. All of it.

"Who are the targets?" he asked.

She told him, mentioned the principals; the McLachlans. A confused look came over his face, she noted, and then a wry grin spread.

"What is it?" she asked. "Is something wrong?"

"Oh, it's nothing. Probably seen it in the newspaper or some such… it isn't important," he said, changing the subject. "However, it would be expensive, what you want. The risk, the planning and all the resources that I would need…"

She shut him down quickly. "Don't concern yourself with that, Mr Smith, I have more than ample funds for this operation." She thought back to the property in Chelsea that she had just sold, one of many she had persuaded her husband to sell from their extensive property portfolio. "Have you ever lost anyone, Mr. Smith? Anyone close? Anyone that matters?"

She watched as the man across from her frowned, almost as if unsure how to answer. She thought she saw pain there. Then the mask washed away from his face and it was all business again. He ignored her.

"And you think this will help, do you? Think this will help you heal?" he asked, changing the subject to distract her.

She shook her head. "No, I don't think I will ever heal, but I think it will satisfy my sense of true justice for my niece and my sister, and if it stops these animals from killing and ruining other innocent people's lives, then in my book it will be justified. They have attacked the wrong people, Mr Smith. I want them to know that."

Gorilla shrugged. He didn't think this little mouse of a woman had it in her. Oh, she had the funds undoubtedly, but did she have the concrete stomach to order the execution of another human being? Grant was keen to find out. "So, you want this Conor McLachlan killed," he said brutally.

She shook her head in the manner of one who hasn't explained herself clearly. "No, you misunderstand me completely...."

Gorilla thought that he had her in that moment. She was already trying to talk herself out of it... backtracking...

She continued. "I want you to destroy the entire organisation. Kill them mercilessly, bring them down. The hierarchy, the soldiers, the bent policeman, their lawyers, their infrastructure. I want their operation, if not destroyed, then at least crippled so that Glasgow police can sweep up the rest. But most of all, I want you, at the end of it all, to put a bullet in Conor McLachlan's head. Do this for me and I will ensure your payment means that you never have to work again. Ever."

And that had been it, spelled out in stark detail. The rest of it had been the pure mechanics of organising a contract. Gorilla

Grant had come out of self-imposed retirement had gathered his team and headed north to destroy a clan of criminals and to execute a murderer.

The clock had been wound. Now it was time to watch the countdown to kill day.

Chapter Nine

The Big Man

Marbella, Spain: 48 hours after the operation in Glasgow...

The big man relaxed on the waterbed, floating gently in the swimming pool of his private villa. An open copy of that month's Playboy lay across the expanse of his fat stomach. A large glass of Sangria rested easily in his hand. His skin was that bright red colour Scotsmen of a certain caste seemed to acquire when they have been exposed to the Mediterranean sun. His father would have called it lobster red.

He hadn't heard from his nephew for the past day or two, which was unlike him. Normally the little fucker was complaining or moaning or wanting to try to take over more parts of the drugs operations. That little bastard was still on probation in Danny McLachlan's eyes, especially after he had topped that wee lassie in Edinburgh during a drunken night out the other year. Christ, the strings he had to pull to get the little bastard off scot free. Threatening witnesses, getting Ollerton to make evidence disappear, payoffs... all bloody kinds of backhanders for his sister's spawn.

Anyway… that was the past. A done deal. Ancient history. He would call back to Glasgow later tonight and give the boyos a rollicking, but today was all about relaxing. Time by the pool, another glass of vino and then maybe later he would see if the housemaid Maria was up for making a little bit of extra money in the bedroom. But that was later, now it was time for a siesta……

He noticed the shadow first. Then he turned his head and blinked through the sunlight to make out, looking down at him from the side of the pool, the shape of a small, well-muscled man in short sleeved shirt, light-coloured slacks and sunglasses. His hands were behind his back. He looked again, knew the face. It was older certainly, but he recognised it nonetheless. A street fight when he was in the Tolly Street Gang more than thirty years ago. He had faced off against a smaller kid with a funny accent. He had been surprised when the smaller kid had bested him. He still wore the scar across his face where the kid had cut him with a straight razor. Then it came to him, the name of the smaller kid, the man that in front of him now. All this passed through his memory in a matter of seconds.

"Who the fuck… hey, I remember you. You're… Jack… Jack Grant? What the fuck are…?

As if on cue, Gorilla Grant brought his hands together out in front of him. They held a semi-automatic pistol with a long, bulbous silencer attached to the end. He fired and the three pops from the silenced pistol came in rapid succession, all to the head of the big man in the pool. The Sangria glass and the blood from the fatal wound all started to seep into the cool blue of the water until eventually the dead body of Fat Danny McLachlan toppled off the waterbed and splashed face down into the pool. He floated like a dead whale, leaving a trail of blood behind him.

Gorilla Grant bent, picked up the empty casings of the bullets and pocketed them. Then he turned and walked calmly away into the setting sun.

THE END

Acknowledgements

Miika and Simone at Creativia for all their fantastic support and hard work.

To Jack, my little Gorilla, for reminding me every day what is important in life. I love you xxx

Finally, to Lulu who, as ever, ALWAYS writes the last line of the Gorilla Grant stories. You do an awesome job of it, girl xxx

A Message from James Quinn

The novella **Gorilla Warfare** is a bit of anomaly in the Redaction stories. It is set way ahead in Gorilla Grant's future. As of the time of writing this, I am barely halfway through writing Book 3; **Rogue Wolves.** I hope readers will bear with me for playing about with the timelines (not that I am overly concerned with timelines... I mean, I'm not Doctor Who... but I am concerned with telling a good story).

This particular story was written in anger. It was written, almost as an experiment, as a release, whilst I was working on an investigation project in the USA during the early part of 2017. It was a frustrating operation and I found that the writing helped me to unwind during those difficult times. Ironically the investigation seemed to have a deeper influence on me than I first thought. The subject matter for both was a mother's grief for a murdered or "lost" or "taken" child. It was a case of real life influencing art.

Kidnapping, especially that of a child, is a heinous crime and is performed by the lowest of the low in my professional and personal opinion, but for the parent left behind wondering what has happened to their loved one, it is only the beginning of a horrendous journey. The mind plays insane tricks. Are they being abused, hurt, scared, and cowering in the dark waiting for the next indignity? For the parent, then comes the drawn-out process of negotiating and dealing with the criminal's manipulative demands of cruelty. His torture can drive even the strongest parents to despair. It is abusive and cowardly. As I say, the lowest of the low.

But...

There is a road back, there is always hope. There are ways for the parents of abducted children to see justice served and to help to keep the fight alive so they can survive and ultimately live again.

Thank you
James Quinn
USA
2017

COMING SOON FROM CREATIVIA PUBLISHING
THE NEW GORILLA GRANT THRILLER

ROGUE WOLVES

He is known as The Master.

He has been at the top of his game for the past thirty years. Spy, double agent, freelance assassin. He has worked for Nazis, Communists, intelligence agencies and terrorists alike. He only operates for big rewards and no one knows his true identity.

But now, the world's most secretive assassin has disappeared, and the intelligence networks of several countries want him captured and interrogated.

Jack "Gorilla" Grant, now a contract agent for the French Secret Service, is assigned the job of bringing The Master down. But more than that, Gorilla has a personal score to settle with his rival, one that could see him up against his most charismatic and lethal foe so far. Gorilla Grant isn't the only player in this game. Hot on his heels is a CIA bounty hunter who is just as deadly as she is beautiful and who is more than capable of hunting down both assassins.

But the Master has an agenda all of his own and is ready to spring a trap that will ensnare the best redactor and bounty hunters in the business… and begin a war that will engulf them all.

About the Author

James Quinn is the author of the Gorilla Grant spy novels. He works as a freelance security consultant and investigator. He has spent nearly two decades in the secret world of covert surveillance, undercover operations and international security.

He is trained in hand to hand combat and in the use of a variety of weaponry including small edged weapons. He is also a crack pistol shot for CQB (Close Quarter Battle) and many of his experiences he has incorporated into his works of fiction.

He lives in the United Kingdom and the USA.

Lightning Source UK Ltd.
Milton Keynes UK
UKHW050203121020
371334UK00023B/387